Shalon DeDiablo illustrated by Lilly Briguglio

One Chilly Night Book 3

DeDiablo, Shalon. Are You Sure?;
illustrations by Lilly Briguglio,
One Chilly Night Series Book 3

Summary: Sophia gets mysterious text
messages while babysitting Liam and Max.
Is she sure they are safe?

ISBN 978-1-7346529-2-5

Chapter One

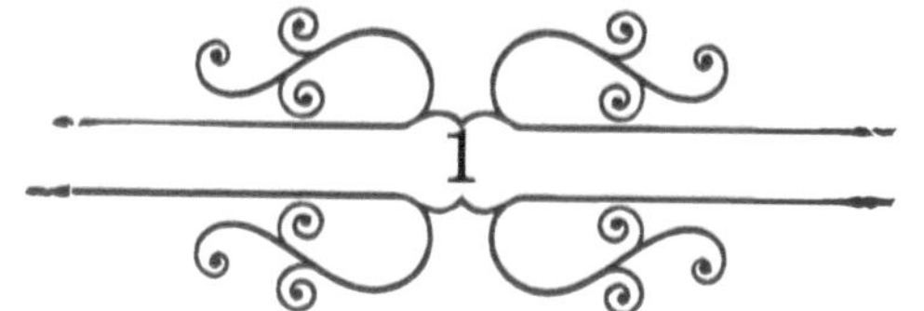

Liam and Max were in the kitchen with their babysitter, Sophia.

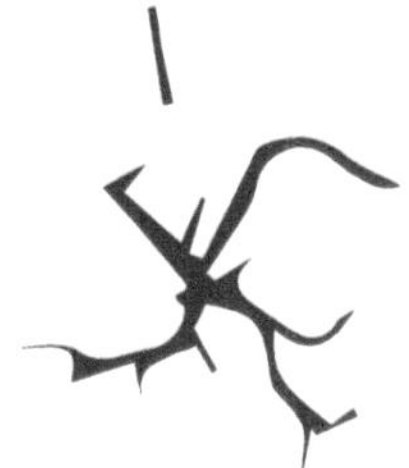

Sophia's phone buzzed.

It was a text from the boys' mother.

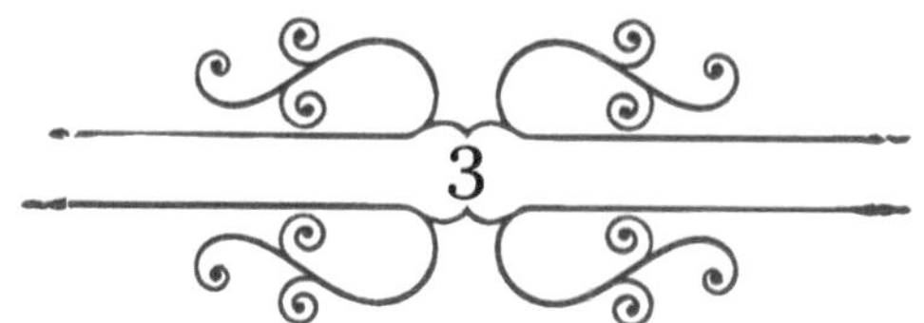

P Mrs Parker

How are the children?

They are fine.

We are eating dinner.

Are you sure?

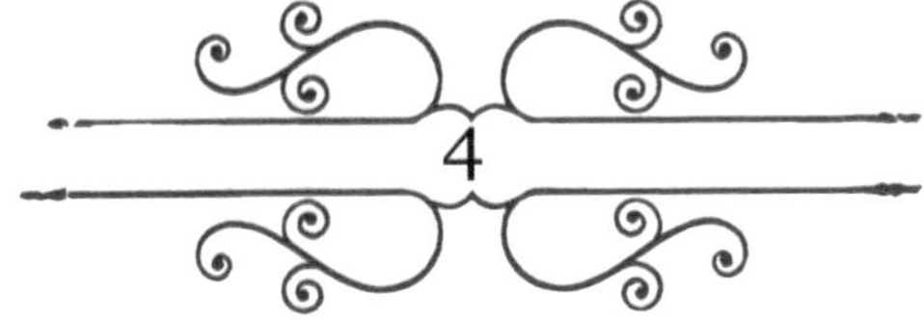

Sophia smiled.

The boys were known for getting into trouble.

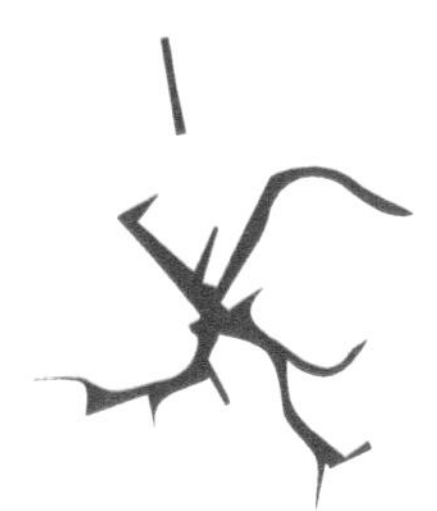

She took a picture of the boys.

"Say cheese!"

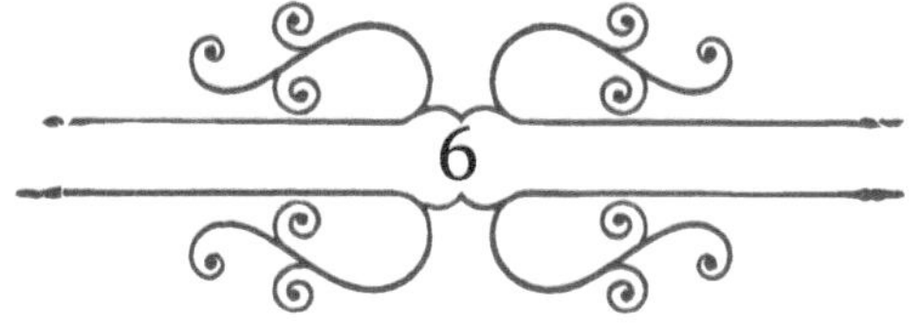

Chapter Two

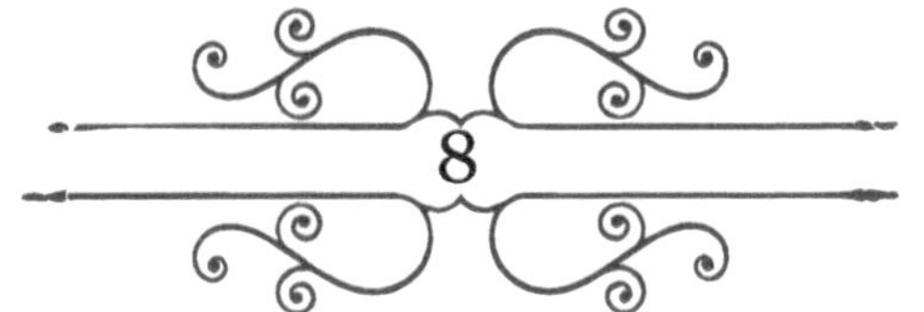

After dinner they watched a movie.

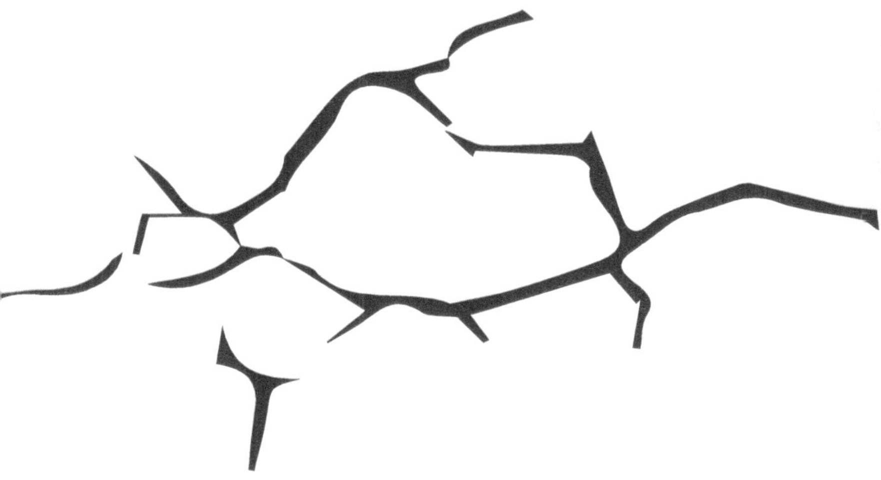

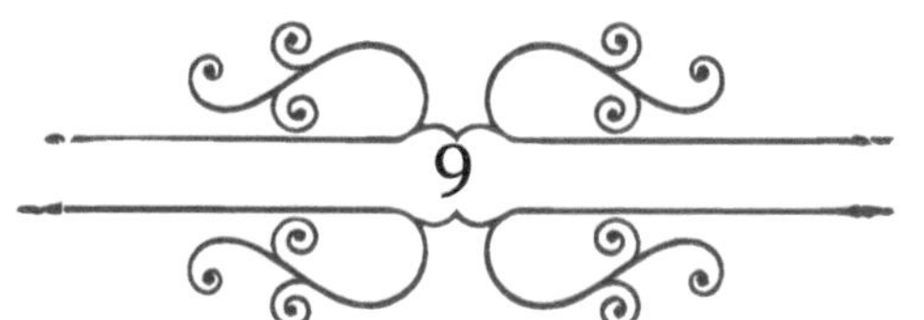

Sophia's phone buzzed again.

It was another text.

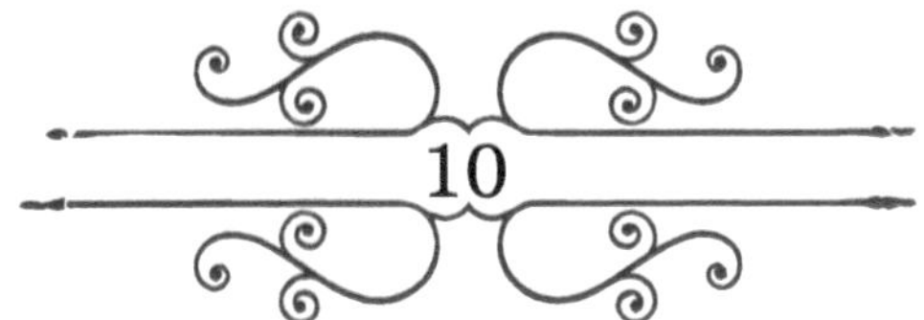

P Mrs Parker

How are the children?

They are fine.

We are watching tv.

Are you sure?

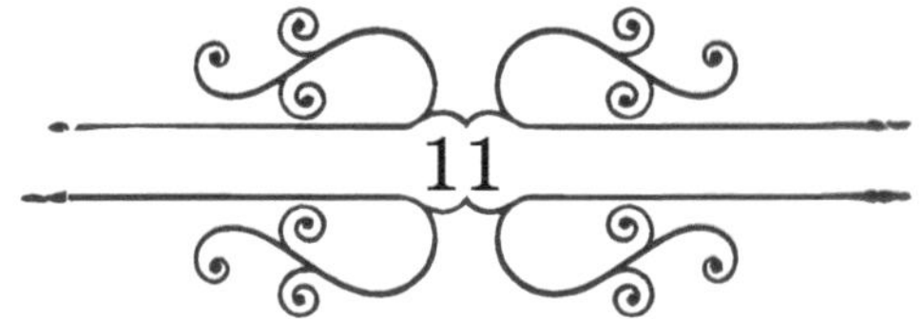

"Your mom must miss you," she told the boys.

"Smile!"

She sent the picture to their mother.

Chapter Three

At bedtime Sophia read the boys a story.

Her phone buzzed again.

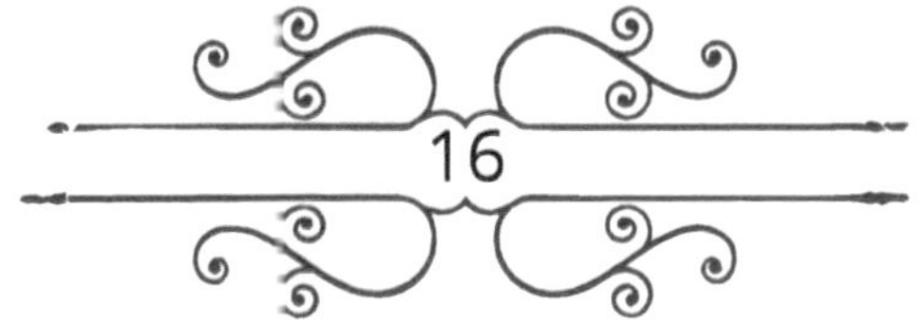

P Mrs Parker

How are the children?

They are fine.

We are reading a story.

Are you sure?

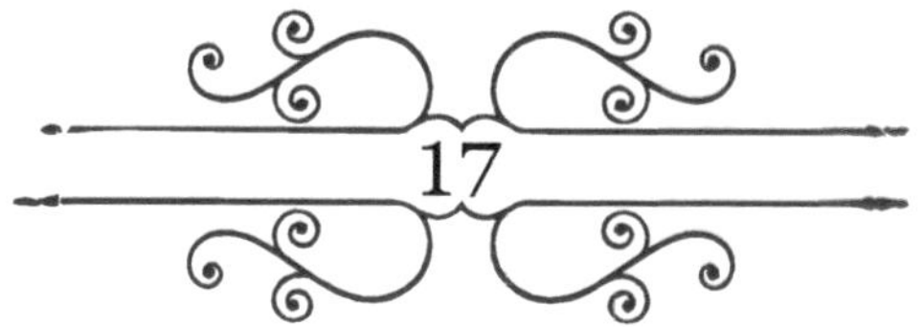

"One last picture for your mom," Sophia said.

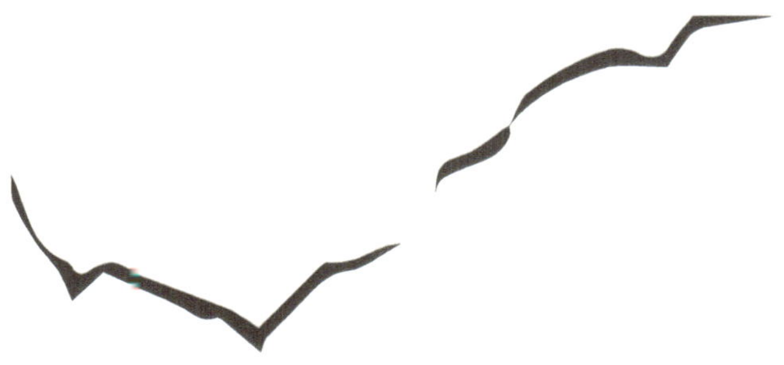

Liam asked, "Why is mom texting so much? She never does that."

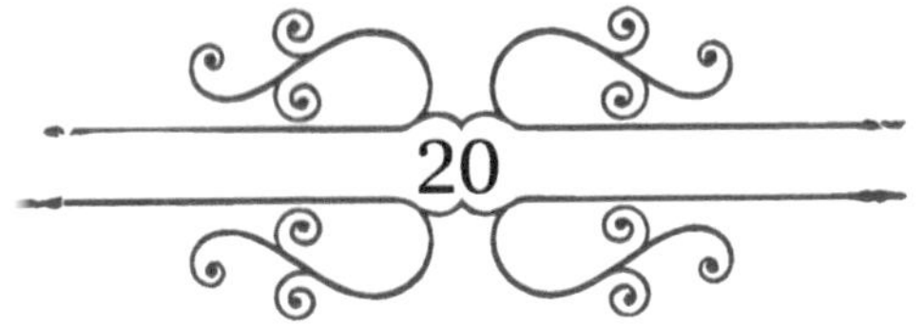

She tucked them in.

"Maybe she misses you."

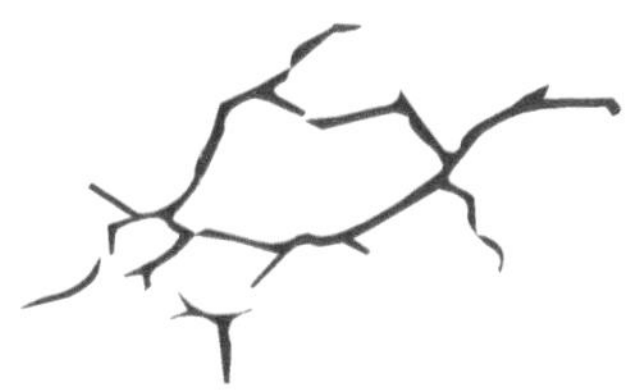

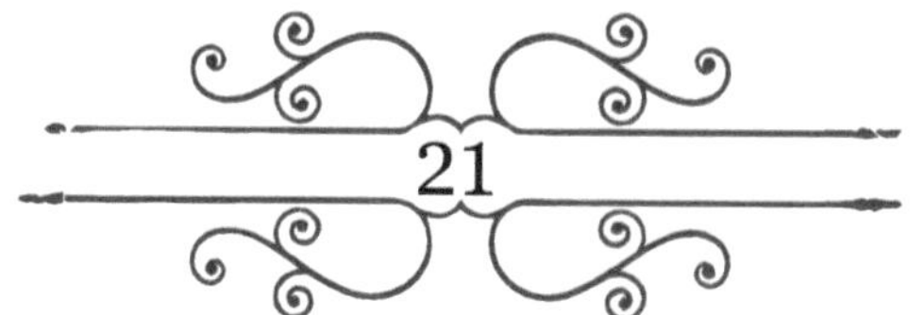

Chapter Four

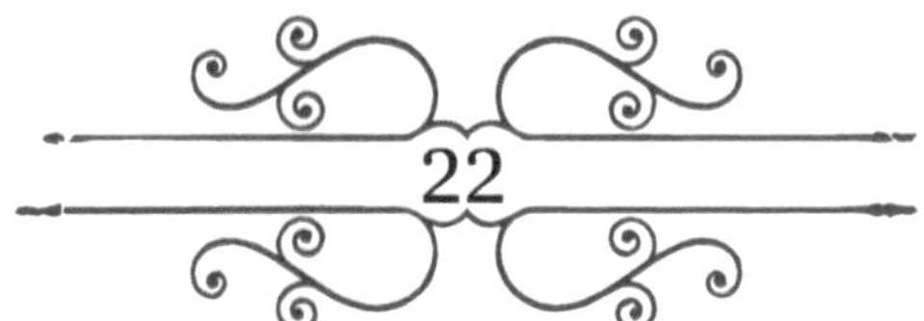

Sophia sat in the chair.

She was reading a book.

Her phone buzzed again.

P Mrs Parker

How are the children?

They are fine.

They are in bed.

Are you sure?

Sophia went upstairs to check on the boys.

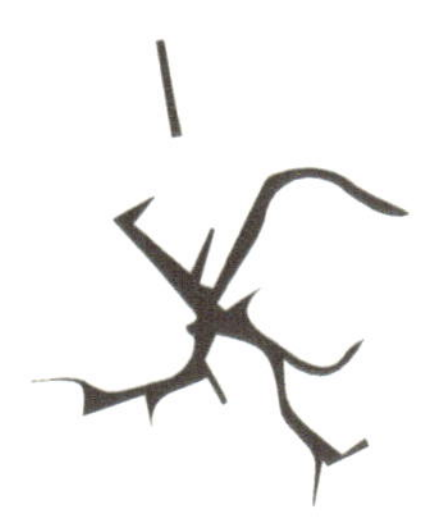

The boys were not in their beds.

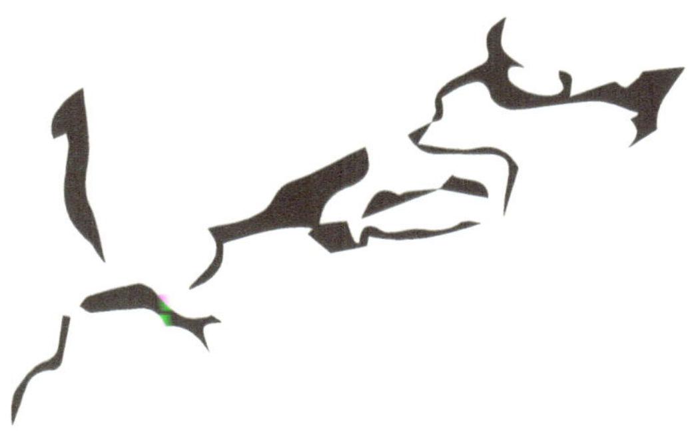

Chapter Five

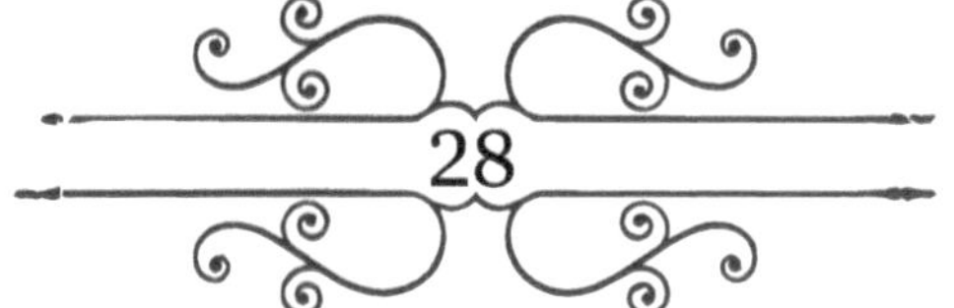

"Very funny boys," Sophia said.

"Stop hiding."

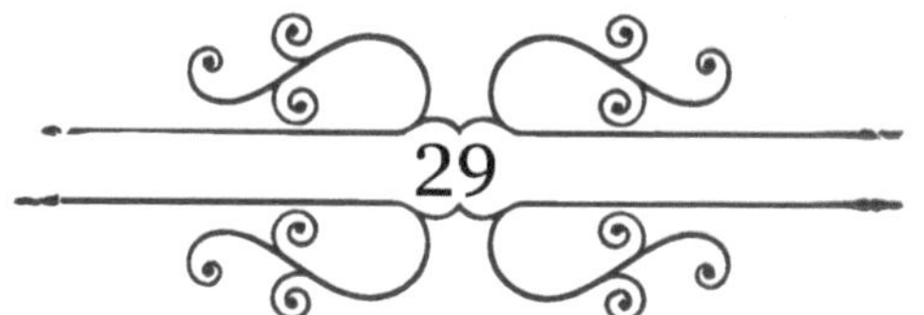

She looked in the closet.

The boys were not in there.

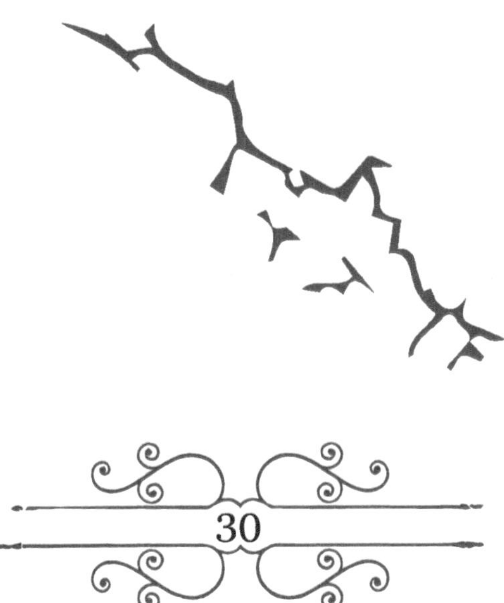

She looked under the bed.

The boys were not there.

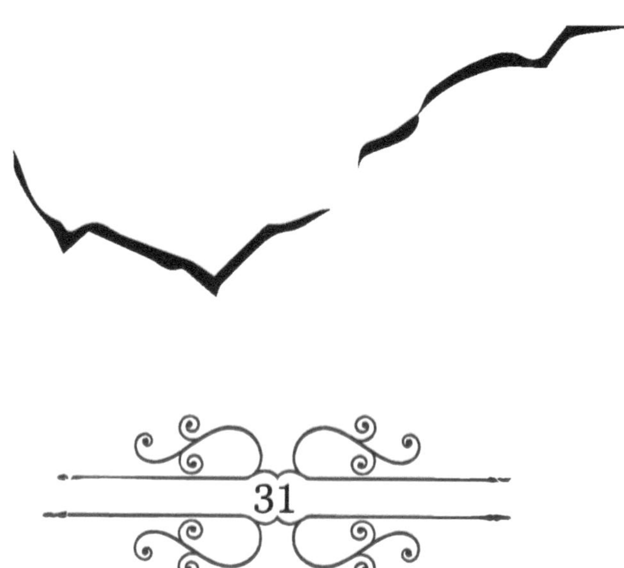

She looked at her hand.

Her hand was wet.

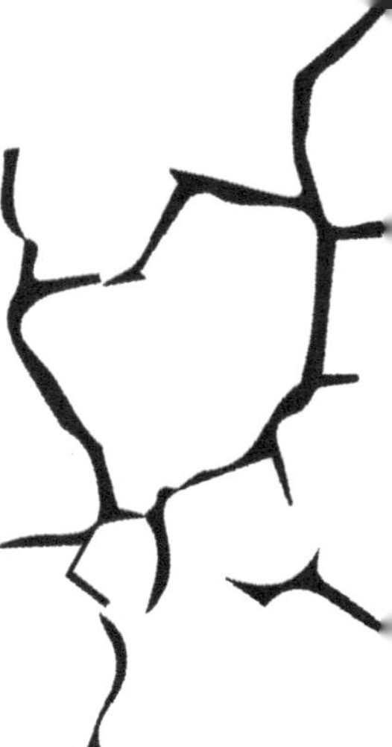

It was blood.

The blood was on the floor!

Sophia ran out of the house.

She called the police.

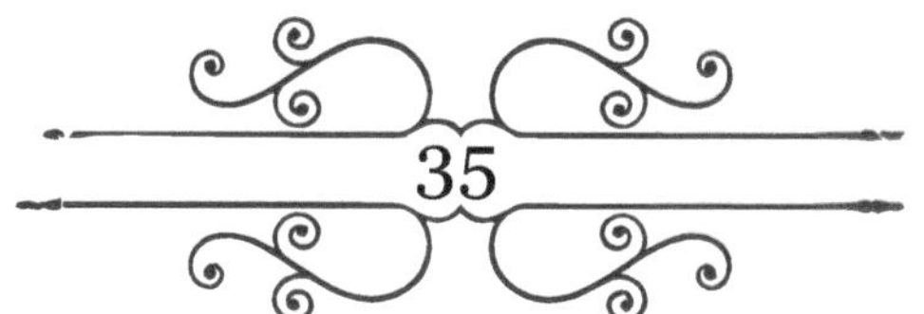

Chapter Six

The police looked for the boys.

They could not find them.

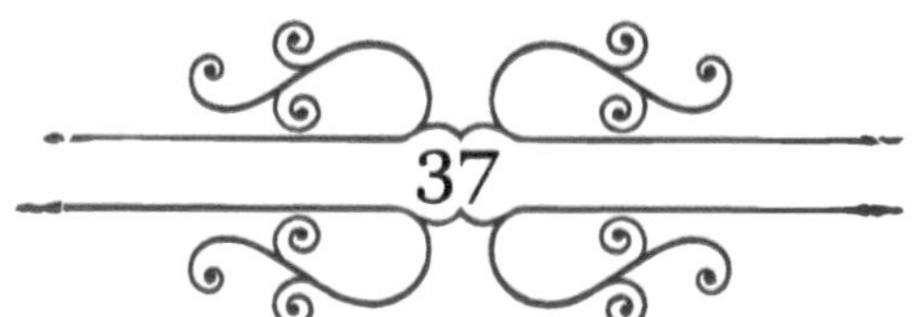

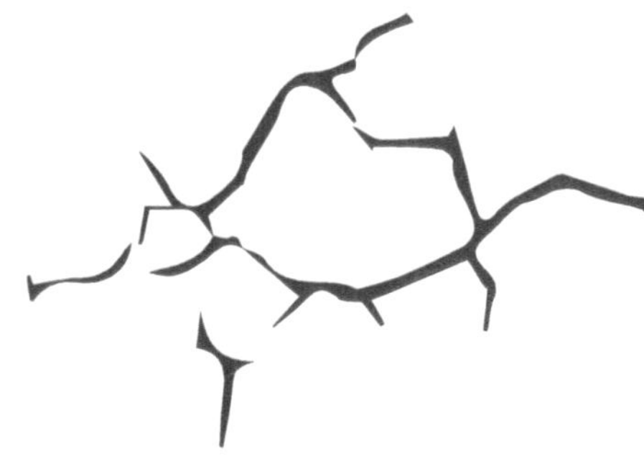

"I checked on the boys like you asked," Sophia told Mrs. Parker

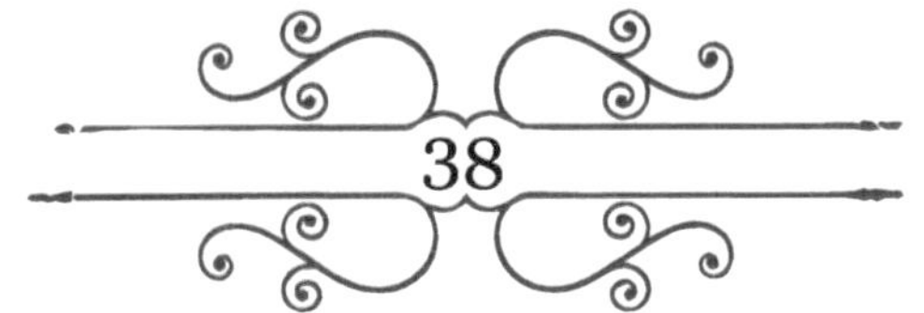

Mrs. Parker said, "I didn't ask you to check on the boys."

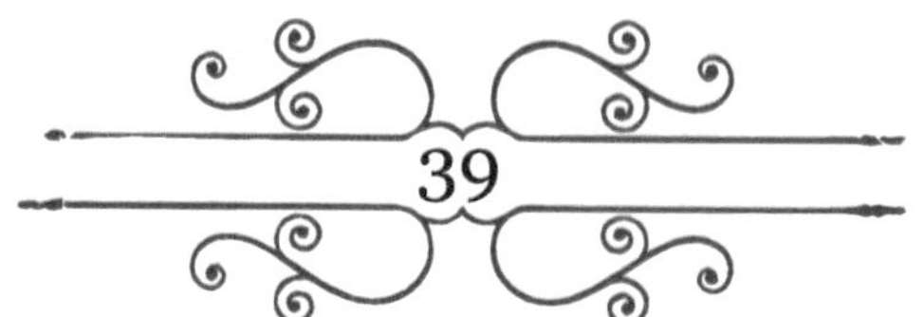

"Yes, you did."

"I have the text on my phone."

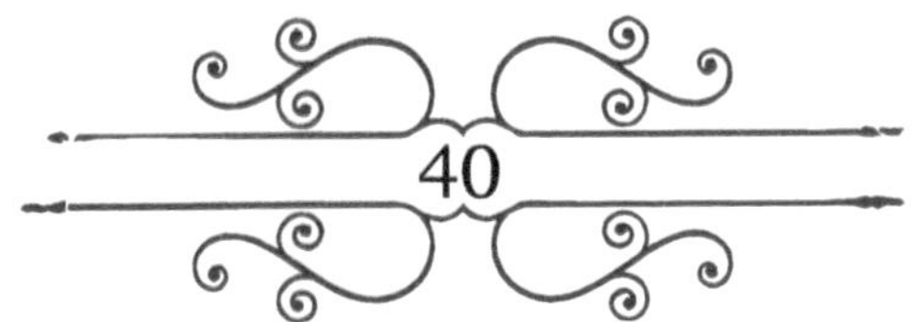

"It was not me," Mrs. Parker said.

"I left my phone in my room."

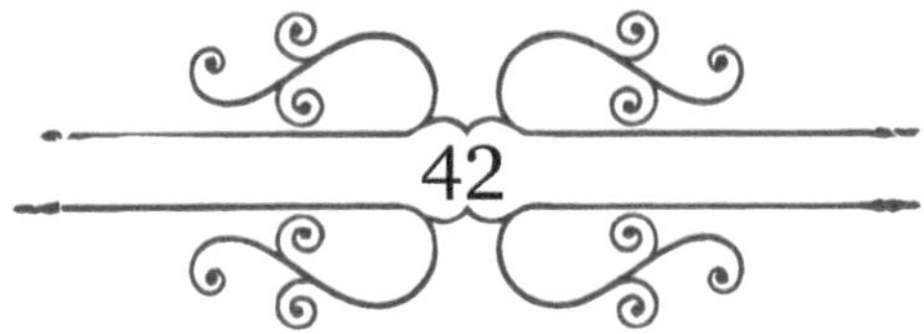

“Then who sent me the texts?”

www.ingramcontent.com/pod-product-compliance
Lightning Source LLC
Chambersburg PA
CBHW030335310726
48979CB00001B/44

* 9 7 8 1 7 3 4 6 5 2 9 2 5 *